THE PUPPY PLACE

RUSTY

THE PUPPY PLACE

Don't miss any of these other stories by Ellen Miles!

THE PUPPY PLACE

RUSTY

ELLEN MILES

SCHOLASTIC INC.

For Nicole, Marc, and Natalie

Copyright © 2019 by Ellen Miles
Cover art by Tim O'Brien
Original cover design by Steve Scott

ISBN 978-1-338-30304-9

10 9 8 7 6 5 4   19 20 21 22 23

Printed in the U.S.A.   40
First printing 2019

CHAPTER ONE

Lizzie Peterson woke up early on the first day of spring vacation. She stretched and yawned, then rolled over to give her puppy, Buddy, a hug. "You're such a good sleeper," she told him as they cuddled. Buddy never snored or stole the covers. He just slept quietly, curled up in a soft, warm ball. He stayed right beside her, ready to snuggle if she woke in the night or had a bad dream. She missed Buddy when he sometimes slept with Charles or the Bean, her younger brothers. Lizzie had dozens of stuffies to hug, but they just weren't the same as a real, live puppy.

Lizzie was crazy about animals, especially dogs of all ages. She loved playing with them, learning about them, and taking care of them. She even had a dog-walking business with three friends. Lizzie stretched and yawned again, thinking how glad she was that they had decided to take a break from the business during school vacation, since they all had big plans.

Lizzie's best friend, Maria, was going to her family's cabin in the woods. Daphne was going to Arizona, and Brianna was going to Disney World. All three of them were super excited and had acted like Lizzie was losing out, since she wasn't leaving town. Lizzie didn't care. She was going to Animal Camp!

"Why do you get to go to Animal Camp every day and I just have to stay home?" Charles asked when she went downstairs that morning. He was sitting at the kitchen table, nibbling a piece of toast.

"I told you," she said as she got herself a bowl of cereal. "Because Ms. Dobbins is just trying out the idea. She decided to start with one four-day session, just for fourth and fifth graders." Lizzie was in fourth, but Charles was only in second grade. "If it works out, they'll have day camp this summer for all ages."

Ms. Dobbins was the director of Caring Paws, the animal shelter where Lizzie regularly volunteered. Ms. Dobbins had been talking forever about hosting an animal day camp, and now she was finally doing it. She and the other staff members at Caring Paws had been planning the camp for weeks, but she hadn't told Lizzie much about it. "I want you to be surprised," Ms. Dobbins had said. "But trust me, there will be a ton of activities and games and plenty of time to be with the animals, too. Plus some special guests. I think you're going to love it."

"Anyway, you get to stay home and play with Buddy," Lizzie reminded Charles. He loved their puppy as much as she did. Sometimes they even argued about who loved Buddy more.

"And with me and the Bean," said Mom as she joined them at the kitchen table with a cup of coffee. "We're going to do some fun things this week, the three of us." She raised an eyebrow at Lizzie. Mom had already told Lizzie that she planned to take Charles and the Bean to a professional hockey game — and she'd even arranged a meeting with the mascot, who was a giant purple tiger. Lizzie knew her brothers were going to love that.

Later, when Mom dropped Lizzie off at Caring Paws, she gave Lizzie a kiss good-bye and said, "Just promise me you won't come home with a puppy for us to foster. I've got enough on my

4

hands already this week; I can't be chasing after a puppy, too."

Lizzie smiled. "No worries," she said. "I already know who I'm choosing for my Pet Pal."

The idea of Pet Pals was the only thing Ms. Dobbins had shared about camp. She'd told Lizzie that each camper was going to have a special friend among the shelter animals, someone they'd take care of, learn about, and maybe even help find a home for. From her volunteering, Lizzie already knew most of the shelter dogs. She had decided she'd choose Nora, an old black Lab who loved to nap in the sun out in the dog yard. Lizzie felt a little sorry for Nora; she had been at the shelter for over six months—very few people wanted to adopt older dogs. But plump old Nora was such a sweetheart, with her gray muzzle and slow, plodding walk. She'd be easy to deal with, too. That would leave Lizzie plenty of time to pay attention to all the other activities at Animal Camp.

"Have fun," Mom said as she gave Lizzie another kiss good-bye.

Lizzie walked into Caring Paws, wondering if she would know any of the other campers. She wasn't usually shy, but it would be nice to see a friendly face.

"Yay! Lizzie's here!" April, one of the shelter staff, gave her a big smile from behind the reception desk. "Camp's starting soon. They're all in the meeting room."

Lizzie smiled and headed to the back. "Wow," she said when she walked in. The room had been transformed from a boring space with a big table and a bunch of chairs into a colorful, exciting place. The table had been pushed against the wall, and huge comfy-looking pillows in every color of the rainbow filled the floor. Posters of animals—from puppies to elephants to tortoises—decorated the walls. Lizzie spotted an array of tempting craft supplies on the table and a stack of T-shirts ready to be passed out to campers. "It looks fantastic in here," she said to Ms. Dobbins, who stood near the door.

Ms. Dobbins smiled happily. "Doesn't it? We're all so excited about camp. We had a lot of fun getting things ready yesterday."

Lizzie saw Nicole, a girl she knew from school, and went to talk to her. A moment later, Ms. Dobbins clapped her hands and asked everyone to grab a pillow and sit in a circle. "Welcome, everyone," she said when they were settled. "We're so happy to have you all here for our very first Camp Cares-a-Lot. For any of you I haven't met yet, I'm Ms. Dobbins, the director of Caring Paws. And I want to introduce Rebecca and Linda, who will be helping with all our activities." She gestured to two teenagers beside her.

Lizzie knew Rebecca and Linda a bit from her volunteering. Linda gave her a little wave, and she waved back.

"We have so many exciting things planned for this week," said Ms. Dobbins, "but we wanted to start with a little icebreaker, just to get to know each other. Let's go around the circle and introduce ourselves, but instead of telling where you live and what grade you are in, tell us which animal you'd be if you could be any animal in the world — and why!"

It was a fun way to get to know people. Lizzie laughed along with everyone else when a girl named Natalie said she'd like to be a monkey so she could swing through the trees, and Lizzie nodded when a boy named Marc said he'd always wanted to be a hawk so he could fly high above the clouds.

Lizzie was not the only one who said she'd like to be a dog, but she was the only one who picked a specific breed: she wanted to be a Newfoundland so she could swim even in the coldest water.

"Wonderful," said Ms. Dobbins when they had each had a turn. "I feel like I really know something about each of you. Now it's time to meet our Pet Pals, the animals you'll be caring for this week. People who are interested in kittens and cats can go with Rebecca. Linda will help you if you want a guinea pig, hamster, or rabbit. And if you're all about dogs"—she gave Lizzie a special wink and a smile—"come with me."

Lizzie jumped right up to follow Ms. Dobbins back to the kennels. She couldn't wait to give Nora a big hug and show the old Lab the special treat she'd brought her.

But as they walked toward the kennels, Ms. Dobbins put her arm around Lizzie's shoulders. "I have a favor to ask you," she said. "We have a new guest here at Caring Paws. He needs some special attention, and I think you're just the person to give it to him. All the other campers are going to be paired with our easiest, most well-behaved dogs — but I'm hoping you'll choose this new guest as your Pet Pal." She stopped at the first kennel. A beautiful dog with a shiny, flowing red coat sprang off his bed and ran to the door of his cage. He put his paws up on the door and barked, wagging his feathered tail. He grinned at Lizzie, his long ears framing a face full of mischievous spirit.

Hi, hi, hi! Let me out so we can play!

"Lizzie, meet Rusty," said Ms. Dobbins.

CHAPTER TWO

"Wow," said Lizzie. "An Irish setter, right? He's beautiful." She held her hand to the wire mesh door of Rusty's kennel so he could sniff it. He snuffled happily and gave her knuckles a lick.

Ms. Dobbins nodded. "Beautiful—and a bit of a handful. And you're right about his breed. The people who relinquished him just couldn't handle that setter energy."

Lizzie knew that "relinquished" meant "gave up." She always hated to hear about people giving up a pet, even though she knew that making such a hard decision was sometimes the right thing to do. "But he's such a happy guy," she said.

It was obvious right away that Rusty was a joyful pup who loved people.

"He is," said Ms. Dobbins. "He's got a terrific spirit. I hear he's also a bit of a mischief maker. He's only a year old, but he's had a few adventures already. You know, running off, eating strange things, that kind of stuff." She touched Lizzie's shoulder. "I need to introduce the other campers to their Pet Pals, and then we're going to take the dogs out into the yard and practice leash manners. Why don't you take Rusty out there first and let him run off some steam before the rest of us come out?"

Lizzie nodded. "Sure," she said. She was flattered to be one of the only kids under fourteen who were allowed to walk the dogs at Caring Paws. She had earned that privilege by showing Ms. Dobbins how responsible she could be, and by following all the rules of the shelter. She knew that dogs were only allowed to run free in the fenced dog yard one at a time unless there was a supervised playtime.

Carefully, she opened the door to Rusty's kennel and slipped inside. She put on his leash, talking to him gently and petting his silky copper-colored coat. "That's a good boy," she murmured as she got ready to walk him down the row of kennels to the outside door.

Rusty pranced about eagerly as she reached for his kennel door. Then he bolted down the aisle, dragging her past Ms. Dobbins and the other campers, who stood in a small group near another dog's kennel. "Whoa!" Lizzie cried. "Easy there, boy." The other campers giggled.

Embarrassed, Lizzie slipped out the door to the dog yard without looking back. She was starting to see what Ms. Dobbins had meant when she called Rusty a handful. "You need to learn some better manners," she told him as she took off his leash.

Rusty grinned up at her and gave a tremendous shake. The silky feathers of his red coat flew out and settled back down.

Who needs manners when you're as good-looking as I am?

Then he took off in a mad dash around the yard, stopping only to sniff and pee now and then as he circled once, twice, three times.

Lizzie watched, shaking her head. What a beautiful dog! His shiny coat rippled in the sunlight. He was thin but strong and athletic, and his long legs seemed to cover half the dog yard's length with every stride. His head had a noble look, with a pointed nose and long, silky ears.

"He's something, isn't he?" Ms. Dobbins had stepped outside to join Lizzie. "I'll help you get him back on the leash. It's not easy to grab him unless you have some treats to offer." She dug into her pocket and pulled out a jerky treat. "Rusty!" she called. "Come, Rusty!"

The red dog ran toward them, then veered off to sniff at a patch of ground.

In a minute. First I have to check on a few things.

Ms. Dobbins shook her head. "Typical teenager," she said. "Always testing to see what they can get away with."

"Teenager?" Lizzie asked.

Ms. Dobbins nodded. "He's about one year old. Dogs are often in a teenager phase when they're about six to eighteen months old." Rusty

was still sniffing. "Rusty!" Ms. Dobbins called again. She held out the treat. "Come see what I have."

Rusty looked up at her.

Oh, right. You're the one with the yummy treats. Okay, maybe I'll join you.

He trotted over, wagging his tail. Ms. Dobbins waited until he sat in front of her with an expectant look on his face. "Good boy," she said, giving him the treat.

Rusty gobbled it down and stood up as if he was about to take off again, but Lizzie stepped forward to put on his leash. When Rusty tried to duck away, she managed to grab his collar. "Got him," she said.

"Good work," said Ms. Dobbins. "I'll go get the other campers."

Lizzie had a few treats in her own pocket, including the big biscuit she had brought for Nora. "Sit, Rusty," she said, holding a treat above his nose. He followed it with his eyes, which automatically made his butt drop so that he was sitting. "Good boy," said Lizzie, giving him the treat.

By the time Ms. Dobbins and the other campers came out into the dog yard, Lizzie had Rusty sitting nicely by her side. Of course, he jumped to his feet as soon as he saw the other dogs parading past.

Hi, hi, hi! Is it playtime now?

Lizzie sighed, but she had to smile. Rusty was so exuberant; who could resist such a joyful personality? Still, as the lesson went on, she couldn't help being a little envious of Nicole, who had chosen Nora as her Pet Pal. The two of them walked easily around the dog yard, Nora plodding peacefully on a loose leash. She didn't pull or veer off to sniff at a rock or try to wrestle with the dog ahead of her. Rusty did all those things and more. He even tried to steal treats out of Lizzie's pocket while Ms. Dobbins showed the campers how to teach their dogs to heel—staying close to a person's left side as they walk together.

Rusty was definitely a handful. But there was something very special about the lanky red pup. With Rusty as her Pet Pal, Lizzie could already tell that Animal Camp was going to be more fun—and a *lot* more challenging—than she ever could have imagined.

CHAPTER THREE

"Nice job, everyone," said Ms. Dobbins. "I can see that you all really love dogs. Your Pet Pals are going to be so happy to see you every day." She checked her watch. "Looks like it's snack time. Let's get our pals settled into their kennels." Lizzie walked Rusty back to his kennel. She told him to sit, then gave him the big biscuit she had brought for Nora. "Good boy," she said as he took it to his bed and began to gnaw it, holding one end down with a big paw while he chewed on the other end. He looked up at her with a goofy grin and thumped his tail happily.

Yum. After this can we go out and play some more?

Lizzie hated to leave Rusty alone in his kennel, even though she knew that the big biscuit would keep him busy for a while. She was already falling in love with the happy guy. "I'll be back later," she promised him as she slipped out the door. Maybe Ms. Dobbins would let her have some extra time with Rusty.

She headed to the meeting room, where Rebecca and Linda were passing out juice boxes and animal crackers for snack. Lizzie found a cushion next to Nicole's and plopped down, sighing.

Nicole laughed. "Are you that tired already? We're only a few hours into our first day of camp."

Lizzie laughed, too. "I know. But dealing with Rusty is kind of exhausting. He's got a lot of energy." She was embarrassed about not being able to control the excitable red dog.

"I noticed," said Nicole. "I know I sure wouldn't be able to handle him. Nora is perfect for me."

That made Lizzie feel a little better. Still, as a dog-walking professional, she thought she should be able to handle any dog.

Ms. Dobbins came over and smiled down at Lizzie. "You did a great job," she said. "I knew you and Rusty would get along."

"But I couldn't even get him to walk nicely on the leash," said Lizzie.

Ms. Dobbins waved a hand. "He won't do it for me, either. He needs a lot of attention and plenty of practice." She smiled again. "Maybe the special guest who's coming this afternoon will have some ideas."

"Who's the special guest?" Lizzie asked.

"A very experienced dog trainer," said Ms. Dobbins. "She's coming to talk to us about how to communicate with dogs."

"Cool," said Nicole.

Lizzie raised her eyebrows. "Does the experienced dog trainer's name happen to be Amanda?" she asked.

Ms. Dobbins laughed. "You guessed it," she said.

Lizzie's aunt Amanda owned a doggy day-care center called Bowser's Backyard. She knew everything there was to know about dogs and dog training. Lizzie was sure Ms. Dobbins was right: if anybody could help Rusty learn to mellow out, it would be Aunt Amanda.

"Maybe she'll have some ideas about how to train Rusty," said Ms. Dobbins. "But right now we've got some other activities planned."

22

After they'd finished their snacks, Rebecca led the campers in a quick game of Obedience School, which was like a dog-themed Simon Says.

"Trainer says, sit!" she said when everyone was lined up in front of her. They all sat. "Shake!" Rebecca said, then smiled, pointing at Marc and Natalie, who'd each held up one "paw." "Uh-uh," she said. "I didn't say 'trainer says'!"

By the time the group had practiced all their "tricks"—rolling over, playing dead, sitting up pretty, and barking on command—Lizzie felt energized again and ready for anything.

After the game, it was time for crafts. "Today we're going to make name tags," said Linda. "Or, as we call them here, dog tags." She held up a piece of construction paper and showed them how she had traced a dog-bone shape onto it, then cut it out. "Or you could make a cat's paw, if that's what you're more into. After you've cut out your shapes, you can decorate them however you like." She gestured to the art supplies laid out on the table.

Lizzie groaned. She was not the most crafty person in the world. She looked toward the door, wondering if she could sneak out and spend some time with Rusty instead. But Nicole pulled Lizzie to the craft table. "Come on," she said. "This'll be fun. What color are you going to choose?"

In the end, Nicole was right. Making the dog tags was fun, and Lizzie was happy with her finished product. Like all the campers' tags, hers had both her name and her Pet Pal's name on it. RUSTY'S PAL, LIZZIE, it said. Lizzie had glued red feathers all around her purple tag—she liked how the feathers represented Rusty's beautiful coat—and sparkled everything up with pink and purple glitter.

"Nice," said Nicole. She showed Lizzie the tag she'd made, with her pal Nora's name in red, surrounded by gold sequins. She'd added some black Lab stickers, too.

Lizzie threaded pink yarn through the holes she'd punched in her tag and put it around her neck. *Rusty's Pal, Lizzie*, she thought. He really did feel like her pal already. She loved his happy attitude. Rusty was overflowing with energy and good spirits. Lizzie knew he must hate being penned up in his kennel all day and overnight.

Would a pal really let a pal live like that?

Lizzie thought back to her conversation with her mom earlier that day.

"Promise me you won't come home with a puppy for us to foster," Mom had said.

"No worries," Lizzie remembered answering.

That wasn't exactly a promise, was it?

25

CHAPTER FOUR

When they finished their craft project, the campers helped clear off the big table for lunch. Lizzie wished she could go hang out with Rusty while she ate the cheese sandwich she'd brought, but Ms. Dobbins shook her head when Lizzie asked.

"Our days are all planned out so everyone will have a great time at camp." She put a hand on Lizzie's shoulder. "Don't worry. You'll have plenty of time with Rusty. I'm so glad you're okay with him being your Pet Pal. I can tell he already likes you a lot."

"I have a feeling Rusty likes just about everyone

he meets," Lizzie said, smiling. Even so, she felt good hearing Ms. Dobbins say that.

Aunt Amanda arrived just as the campers were cleaning up after lunch. Lizzie ran over to give her a hug. "There's the coolest puppy here!" she said. "His name's Rusty, and he's an Irish setter, and—"

Aunt Amanda held up a hand. "I can't wait to meet him, sweetie," she said. "But right now I have to get set up for my presentation. Can you help me pull down the movie screen?" She bustled about, setting her laptop on a stool and plugging it in.

When Aunt Amanda was ready, Ms. Dobbins called for the campers to sit on the floor. "And now for today's special guest," she said, "who happens to be related to one of our campers!" She explained that Amanda was Lizzie's aunt and told everyone about her doggy day-care business.

"Amanda is here to help us learn to speak dog language," she said. She laughed. "I don't mean we can translate exactly what they're saying when they bark or whine. It's more about learning to read their body language, right, Amanda?"

"That's right. We can tell a lot about how dogs are feeling by looking at the way they are standing, or how they're holding their ears and tails. Can anybody guess why that's important?" Aunt Amanda asked. She looked around for raised hands.

Lizzie waved hers. "Because," she said when her aunt called on her, "it's good to be able to know how a dog is feeling. Like if he's friendly, or worried or scared. Then you know how to act with the dog, like whether to pet him or leave him alone."

Aunt Amanda nodded. "Exactly. Knowing how to speak Dog is helpful when we meet strange dogs and also for communicating with our own dogs. Let's look at some pictures and see how well we can read dog body language." She pushed a button on her clicker, and a picture of a golden retriever filled the screen. The dog was sitting with her tail along the floor. Her mouth was slightly open, her ears were hanging naturally, and her eyes were bright. "What do we think about this dog?" she asked. "Is she angry or upset?"

"No!" everybody yelled.

"Happy!" Marc said.

"Relaxed," said another camper.

"Very good," said Aunt Amanda. "That's a dog who's ready to interact and play." She clicked again and showed them a picture of a Dalmatian lying on his back with his paws in the air. "How about this one?"

"That dog does not want to fight," said Natalie.

"Exactly," said Aunt Amanda. "We call this submissive. He's showing that he is not a threat.

Some dogs may do this when they're feeling uncomfortable and need space. Other dogs might be looking for a belly rub. It's best to hold off on that unless you know the dog well."

"My puppy, Buddy, loves belly rubs," Lizzie whispered to Nicole.

"My dog, Sandy, does, too," Nicole whispered back.

Aunt Amanda moved to the next picture. It was of a German shepherd who was crouching low with his ears back and his head turned away. His tail was between his legs. "And this dog?" she asked.

"Scared!" someone said.

"Worried," said Nicole.

"Upset," said another camper. "Maybe even mad."

Aunt Amanda nodded. "You're all right. When a dog crouches low, he might be angry. But see the way this dog's head is turned away and his tail is tucked? Because of that, we can guess that he is more afraid or confused than angry. He is showing stress, and it's probably best to leave him alone unless you are his owner. He needs a calming word or touch from someone he knows and loves." She moved to another picture, of a dog yawning wide.

"Sleepy!"

"Bored!"

Nobody was bothering to raise their hands anymore. Everyone yelled out ideas.

"Maybe," said Aunt Amanda. "But yawning can also be a sign of stress. So can panting, or pacing, or even drooling." She showed some more slides, including a scary one of a dog with all her teeth bared, and talked about how important it was to notice the signals dogs were giving all the time. "For example, pay attention the next time you hug your dog. Does he turn his head away? Does she lean in the other direction or lay her ears back? Not all dogs enjoy being hugged."

"My dog hates hugs," said one of the campers. "She likes to play with her sock monkey toy, though. So we do that instead."

"Great," said Aunt Amanda. "It sounds like you know how to communicate really well with your dog." She clicked to one last slide, of her own dogs: four pugs and a big golden retriever, all lined up on her big brown couch. She introduced each of them by name, ending with Bowser, the golden retriever her business was named after. "My guys said to say hi to all of you. They're really excited that you're learning to speak Dog."

Ms. Dobbins stood up and started clapping, and everyone else joined in. "Thank you, Amanda. That was wonderful. Maybe you'll come back another day and share some more of what you know about dogs."

Ms. Dobbins smiled at the campers. "What a great first day of camp," she said. "I hope you all had fun and learned some things about animals." She checked her watch. "Your parents will be here to pick you up in about fifteen minutes. Come on up and take a camp T-shirt, then you can pack your things and get ready."

All the campers rushed to the big table, where stacks of Camp Cares-a-Lot T-shirts were laid out according to size and color. Lizzie quickly picked out a red one, then grabbed her backpack and waited impatiently while Aunt Amanda put her computer away and chatted with Ms. Dobbins. Lizzie really, really wanted her aunt to meet Rusty. She knew that if anyone could help her talk her mom into fostering the feisty red pup, it would be Aunt Amanda.

CHAPTER FIVE

"Can you text my mom and ask her to pick me up a little later?" Lizzie asked Aunt Amanda as they walked toward the kennels. "I really need some training help with Rusty." She had decided not to talk about her fostering idea right away. First she wanted her aunt to meet Rusty. She wanted to see what Aunt Amanda thought of him.

"Sure." Aunt Amanda pulled out her phone and clicked away. "Now, where is this amazing puppy you want me to meet?"

"Right here," said Lizzie, stopping in front of Rusty's kennel. The red pup leapt to his feet as soon as he saw her. He shook off and ran to the door of his kennel. He put a paw up on the wire mesh and gave a happy bark.

It's you again! I knew you'd come back. I've been so bored. Is it time to play again?

"Hi, Rusty," said Lizzie, putting her hand up next to his paw. "Uh-oh," she added when she noticed the pile of shredded fleece that had once been Rusty's bed. "I think somebody was bored."

Aunt Amanda smiled and shook her head. "Irish setters can be a handful," she said. "They have a lot of energy, and they need a lot of attention."

Lizzie slipped inside Rusty's cage so she could pet him. He wriggled happily as she scratched between his long, silky ears. "But I think he's really smart, too," she said. "And he's such a happy guy."

"He's gorgeous," said Aunt Amanda. "Look at that coat."

Lizzie snapped a leash onto Rusty's collar. "Yup, he's gorgeous," she said. "But he doesn't seem to know how to walk nicely on a leash."

"We can work on that," said Aunt Amanda. She slipped a hand into her pocket and pulled out a bag of treats. Rusty rushed over to sniff at it through the mesh of his kennel. "That's right," said Aunt Amanda. "I've got some special goodies here."

They took Rusty out to the dog yard. "Let's let him run a little first," suggested Aunt Amanda. "He's got a lot of energy to burn off."

Rusty took off at a mad gallop the second Lizzie unclipped his leash. He dashed around and around the yard, ears flapping in the wind.

Wheee! It feels so good to run.

As Rusty was about to pass them for the third time, Aunt Amanda held out the bag of treats. "Come see what I have, Rusty," she said.

Rusty put on the brakes and slid to a stop, grinning up at her.

Yup, yup, I know you've got something good! I can smell it already.

Aunt Amanda told him to sit, and he plopped right down, still staring up at her. "Good boy," she said, tossing him a treat. She smiled at Lizzie. "I've never met a dog who can resist my friend Sue's homemade jerky treats."

Rusty had gulped down the treat and was still watching Aunt Amanda. "Good boy," she said again. "Look at me. That's good. Look at me." She waited until he was gazing into her eyes again and gave him another treat. "The first step for teaching a dog like Rusty to walk nicely on a leash is getting his attention," Aunt Amanda said as she snapped on Rusty's leash. "He has to feel like you're the most interesting thing in the world. Good treats can really help!"

Aunt Amanda patted her leg. "Come on, Rusty, let's walk," she said. Rusty started right off with her but soon pulled forward until he was straining at the leash. Aunt Amanda stopped moving. Rusty turned back to see what was going on. "Good boy!" she said. "Look at me!" She gave him a treat. Again, she turned to Lizzie. "Now I'm rewarding him just for checking in with me. Soon he'll get the picture—that he should be paying attention to me all the time."

Sure enough, within a few minutes, Aunt Amanda was moving around the yard with Rusty walking calmly at her side. He was like a different dog! Rusty seemed to be really enjoying himself. His long, feathered tail wagged constantly as he walked next to Aunt Amanda. He gazed up at her lovingly as he pranced along, waiting for praise and treats.

What do you want me to do next? Just tell me. I'll do anything for some attention—and some more of those treats.

Lizzie was amazed. She had seen her aunt work with a lot of different dogs, but she'd never seen her make such a difference so quickly. "Rusty really is smart, isn't he?" she asked.

Aunt Amanda nodded. "He is. And he wants to please. He really likes to be praised, and he'll do just about anything you ask once he understands what you want."

"I knew it," said Lizzie. "I knew he had a lot of potential. All he needs is a little attention, and he'll turn into a dog that anybody would want to adopt." She took a deep breath. "That's why I hope you can help convince my mom that we should foster him."

Aunt Amanda laughed. "Aha!" she said. "I had a feeling that's where this was going."

"So did I," Mom said, stepping out of the shadows near the door to the dog yard.

"Have you been watching the whole time?" Lizzie asked.

"Just about," Mom said. "Ms. Dobbins sent me out here. She told me that you're already head over heels for this dog." She put her hands on her hips. "He's beautiful. I can see why you like him, but, Lizzie, I thought we talked about this. You promised you wouldn't beg me to foster a puppy you met during camp."

"Well, I didn't exactly promise," Lizzie began. She could see from her mom's face that this argument wasn't going to get her anywhere, so she moved on. "But anyway, Rusty wouldn't be any trouble for you. He'll just stay with us at night, and during the day he'll come to Caring Paws with me." She held her breath, waiting to see what Mom would say.

CHAPTER SIX

"Look at them go!" said Charles as he and Lizzie stood in the backyard later that day. Rusty and Buddy tore around the yard, chasing each other so fast that sometimes one or the other of them almost somersaulted as they took a turn. Rusty's coat was a red blur.

Mom had given in to fostering Rusty—at least, she'd agreed to give it a try. Mom always gave in when it came to fostering puppies. With some puppies it took a little more work, but in the end she never really put her foot down and said no. It had helped that Aunt Amanda had gotten to know Rusty a little bit. "He's really a good boy at heart," she had told Lizzie's mom as she and Lizzie hurried her past his kennel at Caring Paws. (Neither of them had wanted Mom to spot the shredded dog bed.) "He'll get along great with Buddy, and I don't think he'll be much trouble at all."

Ms. Dobbins had helped, too. "You're doing me—and Rusty—a huge favor," she said as she saw them out the door. "I think he'd be so bored here overnight. Also, the more time he can spend with a family, the better. He'll learn some manners at your house, and soon he'll be ready for adoption."

"Well, we'll see how it goes tonight and take it from there," Mom said. She turned to Lizzie. "And don't forget: you're in charge of him."

"I promise," Lizzie said. This time it really was a promise. She was eager to spend more time with Rusty and see what he could learn.

Now, in the backyard, she smiled as she watched Rusty and Buddy play. This was what he really needed: a chance to run, to have fun, to let loose some of that wild energy. She grinned as she saw him shake off, sprawl into a play bow with his paws outstretched, then take off again with Buddy chasing after him. She had a feeling Rusty would sleep well that night, with all the running and wrestling.

But Rusty surprised her. Even after all that fun, the red pup seemed full of mischief. Back in the house, he was into everything. First he pulled every single toy out of Buddy's toy basket. Then he started dragging the couch pillows onto the floor. He got into the dog food, spilled a water dish all over the kitchen floor, shredded a magazine Mom had left on the coffee table, and stole the Bean's special blankie. "Rusty, no!" Lizzie kept saying as she followed him around.

Rusty really was a handful. But that night, he curled up on Lizzie's bed, put his head on her belly, and gazed up at her adoringly as she stroked his silky ears.

That was the most fun day ever! I'm really glad we're pals.

Her heart melted. He wasn't a *bad* dog—in fact, he was one of the sweetest pups she'd ever met. He couldn't help that he was just bursting with energy and high spirits. "Aw, Rusty," she said. "My pal."

The next morning, when Mom dropped Lizzie and Rusty off at Caring Paws, she reminded Lizzie that they'd agreed to take Rusty for only a night to see how it went. "If he's too much for you, I'm sure Ms. Dobbins will understand."

Lizzie shook her head. "I can handle him. I want Rusty to stay with us until we find the perfect new owner for him," she said. "Gotta take care of my pal!" She kissed her mom good-bye, hopped out of the car, and led Rusty into Caring Paws.

Lizzie did not need Aunt Amanda to translate what Rusty was saying when she put him back into his kennel that morning. He looked up at her with big, sad eyes. He held one ear out at a pitiful angle, while the other drooped. His tail drooped even more. He slowly lifted a paw, as if to wave a sad good-bye. Rusty's whole body was speaking to Lizzie.

What? You're not really leaving me here, are you? I thought we were pals.

Lizzie swallowed back a lump of guilt. "I'll see you soon," she told him. "Remember? You're my Pet Pal. And you'll come home with me again

46

tonight and hang out with Buddy and Charles and the Bean, and—"

"Lizzie, we're starting," called Ms. Dobbins from the door to the dog area. She stepped in for a moment to see Rusty. "Aww, he's really working it, isn't he? Only a dog can make you feel that guilty."

Lizzie nodded, swallowing again. She gave Rusty one last scratch through the wire mesh, then followed Ms. Dobbins to the meeting room.

The morning went by fast, with crafting time (they made scratch pads for the shelter cats and kittens), games (animal tag and another round of Obedience School), and snack. Lizzie enjoyed herself, but she never stopped thinking about Rusty.

Finally, it was Pet Pal time. Lizzie practically ran to the kennels, and she and Rusty had a happy reunion. Again, she took him out alone to the dog yard so he could run. Then everyone else came out and it was time for leash walking. Lizzie was prepared with extra-tasty treats and everything she remembered from what Aunt Amanda had shown her.

Ms. Dobbins was impressed. "He's doing so much better already," she said. "I knew you'd be the perfect pal for Rusty."

After leash walking, the campers spent some time learning how to groom their dog pals. Ms. Dobbins handed out brushes and combs and explained the best ways to get rid of shed hair and undo a knot from a long coat. She walked around to each Pet Pal pair in turn, helping the campers work with their dogs. "One of our vet techs is going to demonstrate proper toenail clipping tomorrow," she told them, "on Meet the Vet Day. You'll also see how the vet gives an injection and how they do stitches."

She stopped in front of Lizzie. "He looks beautiful," she said. Rusty's silky red coat was gleaming from the brushing Lizzie had given him. "We have a family coming to look at him tomorrow, and I'm sure they'll be impressed."

"Really?" Lizzie asked. "A family wants to adopt Rusty?" She felt her stomach drop. She wasn't sure she was quite ready to give him up. No matter how many dogs her family fostered, Lizzie could never get used to that part of it.

"Well, they want to adopt a dog," said Ms. Dobbins. "They'll look at all the dogs we have here. But right now, I'd say Rusty is pretty irresistible. And he could be perfect for a family with a bunch of kids. He'd get all the playtime and attention he needs."

Lizzie nodded and bit her lip. "Great," she said. "I hope they like him." But inside, she was thinking, *Too soon! Too soon!*

CHAPTER SEVEN

All during lunch, Lizzie had a knot in her stomach. Was somebody really going to adopt Rusty so quickly?

"That would be a good thing, wouldn't it?" asked Nicole. "I mean, isn't that kind of the point here? To find great homes for these animals?"

Lizzie shrugged. "Yeah," she said. "It is. Of course it is. I know that. But I just wanted a little more time with Rusty. He's so much fun! All he wants to do is play." She bit into one of the chocolate-chip cookies Linda had brought for a special treat. It was sweet and gooey and delicious, but she hardly tasted it. Suddenly, she just wanted the camp day to be over so she could take Rusty home and watch him zoom around the yard with Buddy again. What mischief would Rusty get into tonight? You just couldn't predict with a puppy like that.

"Cheer up, Lizzie," said Ms. Dobbins as she walked by. "I think you're really going to like today's special guest."

Lizzie nodded glumly. "Who's coming?" she asked, just to be polite.

"It's a surprise. You'll see. We'll be heading out to meet her in the dog yard in a few minutes, as soon as lunch is done and we're all cleaned up."

Lizzie perked up a little. At least if they were going out to the dog yard, she'd be passing by Rusty's kennel. She could say hi and give him a pat, and—"Can Rusty come out with us?" she asked. "Please, please, please? I'll keep a really close eye on him and he won't be any trouble."

Ms. Dobbins was shaking her head. "I don't think that would work out too well. You'll see why when you meet our guest."

Lizzie couldn't guess what that might mean. "If I'm all done with my lunch, can I go say hi to Rusty until we go out to the dog yard?"

Ms. Dobbins smiled at her. "You've really fallen for that guy, haven't you?" she asked. "I can see why. He's a special dude." She gave Lizzie a pat on the shoulder. "Go ahead. And give him a kiss for me."

Lizzie ran for the kennels. "Hey, boy," she said as she let herself into Rusty's kennel. "I missed you!" She ruffled his ears, and Rusty kissed her face.

She sat on the bench inside his kennel and picked up a chew toy he'd left beneath it. "Wanna play?" she asked, dangling it in front of his nose.

Rusty pawed at the toy, giving a happy little yip.

52

Of course I want to play. I always want to play!

Too soon, Ms. Dobbins came through the kennels, leading all the campers to the dog yard. "Time to go, Lizzie," she said. "I promise it will be worth it."

When they got to the yard, Lizzie saw a sleek black-and-white border collie sitting calmly next to a woman dressed in a cowgirl costume. "Wow," said Lizzie.

"Yeah, her outfit is amazing," said Nicole. The woman wore a red-and-white silk blouse and skirt, both decorated with red fringe. She also had on a red cowboy hat and the fanciest pair of sparkly red cowboy boots Lizzie had ever seen.

"I'm not talking about her outfit," said Lizzie, even though she liked it a lot. "I'm talking about the dog. Did you ever see a border collie sit so quietly? They're usually zooming around like crazy. They have even more energy than Rusty!" Lizzie could tell right away that this woman must be really good at training dogs.

"Hi, everyone," said the woman, waving to the campers as they found places to sit around the edges of the dog yard.

Ms. Dobbins went to hug her. "This is Laureen," she said. "She's here to demonstrate a very special sport that she does with her dog, Astro."

Lizzie saw one of Astro's ears twitch when he heard his name, but other than that, he didn't move a muscle.

"Has anyone heard of freestyle?" Laureen asked.

Lizzie frowned. That sounded familiar, but she couldn't remember exactly what it was.

"Some people call it dancing with dogs," Laureen said.

"Oh!" said Lizzie. Now she remembered hearing about it. Maybe Aunt Amanda had mentioned it. "Cool."

Laureen smiled. "Astro and I have been training together for about five years now. We've
competed all over the country, and we even went
to an international competition in Sweden last
year. We work really hard, but we also have a
whole lot of fun. I think you'll be able to tell how
much Astro loves to dance." She nodded to Ms.
Dobbins. "I guess we're ready to start," she said.

Ms. Dobbins turned the music on. It was a song
that Lizzie recognized, a hokey cowboy tune her
dad liked to sing. Laureen stood up straight. She
moved one of her hands the tiniest bit, and Astro
stood up on his hind legs and began to spin
around.

The campers gasped.

"Whoa!" said Lizzie.

Next Laureen gave another tiny signal, and
Astro ran toward her. Laureen began to walk
slowly, taking long steps, while Astro looped

beneath her legs and around her body, doing figure eights around her while she moved. She
stopped, held up a hand, and sent him away from
her—walking backward!

Lizzie shook her head in awe. She had never,
ever seen a dog do the things Astro was doing.
And Laureen didn't even have to say a word to
him. It really was like they were dancing together.
They got closer and moved apart. Laureen spun
while Astro ran in circles around her, like a moon
orbiting a planet. No matter what else he was
doing, Astro stared up at Laureen's face with full
concentration, watching her closely.

Lizzie nodded to herself. This was what Aunt
Amanda meant by "attention." Astro was paying
attention with every bit of himself. It was like
nothing in the world existed except for Laureen.
A hot-air balloon could have landed in the dog
yard and he probably wouldn't even have noticed.

"Wow," Lizzie breathed again as the song came to an end. Laureen knelt down and held her arms in a big circle, and Astro leapt through them, then turned and leapt through again. Then Laureen stood up, and she and her dog each took a bow. As the campers applauded, Laureen held out her arms. Astro jumped into them, and she hugged him close.

"That was amazing, wasn't it?" asked Nicole.

Lizzie just nodded. She couldn't even speak. All she could think about was how much she wanted to learn to do freestyle—with Rusty.

CHAPTER EIGHT

"Back up, back up!" Lizzie held up her hand, palm forward, in Rusty's face.

He wagged his feathery tail, gave his whole body a good shake, and offered Lizzie his paw.

Did you want to shake hands? I'm confused, but I'll do whatever you want.

Lizzie rolled her eyes. "No, not 'shake,'" she said. "'Back up' means go backward." How did Laureen *do* it? Lizzie had taught a lot of dogs how to do a lot of things, but she couldn't figure out how to get Rusty to understand what she wanted him to do.

As soon as she'd gotten home from camp, Lizzie had headed out to the backyard with Charles and the dogs. Buddy wanted to be part of the lesson, too. He offered his paw, rolled over, and sat up pretty, showing off all the tricks he knew—but he didn't seem to know how to go backward, either.

"Maybe if I show them," Charles said. "Pretend I'm a dog, and give me the command." He held up his hands like paws, waiting for Lizzie's order.

Lizzie laughed. "That's not going to work," she said. "But why not? Let's try anyway." She snapped her fingers to get both puppies' attention. "Ready?" she asked Charles. She held up her hand in front of Charles. "Back up!"

Charles began to walk backward, still holding up his hands like paws. The dogs watched him with interest, tails wagging.

"Be careful!" said Lizzie. "You're just about to—"

Charles tripped over a flowerpot and fell. Both dogs rushed over to lick his face. He threw his arms over his head, giggling. "Cut it out, you guys," he said as the puppies nosed at him. He struggled to his feet, pushing them away. "Do you think they got it?" he asked.

Lizzie shook her head. "Honestly? No. But I'll try again. Here, Rusty!" She patted her thigh, and the red pup came running. At least he knew his name and usually came when he was called. That was something.

She watched Rusty's beautiful coat ripple in the sunshine as he ran, and she thought about how great he would look dancing with her, in front of a huge audience. Lizzie could just picture Rusty twirling and leaping the way Astro did. Maybe he was a little big for the leaping-into-her-arms finale, but he could do everything else. What song would she choose for them to dance to? Lizzie hummed a favorite tune.

"Okay, Rusty," she said when he was standing in front of her. "Let's try again." She held up a hand. "Back up." This time, she took a step forward, toward him. Rusty looked up at her and took a step back. "Good! Good boy!" said Lizzie. "That's it!"

Rusty wagged his tail so hard that his whole body wagged, then he jumped up on Lizzie, planting his paws on her chest.

Yay! I made you happy. That's all I really want to do.

"Uh-uh, Rusty. Off! No jumping." Lizzie couldn't help laughing as she stepped away. Maybe one step backward was as much as she was going to get in one training session. She couldn't imagine how long it must have taken Laureen to teach Astro all the moves he did so perfectly.

After dinner that night, Lizzie asked her mom to help her look for freestyle videos online. Ms. Dobbins had told her that there were lots. They went up to Mom's office and started to do some research on her computer.

"Look! It's Laureen," said Lizzie, pointing to one of the thumbnail pictures. "Play that one."

They both leaned forward to watch as Laureen and Astro entered a large open ring in a big arena full of people. The announcer gave their names, and Laureen and Astro took a bow, then stood apart, perfectly still, until the music began.

Astro looked the same as he had that day at camp, but this time Laureen was dressed in a '50s-style outfit like the ones in the movie *Grease*. She wore a pink sweater, black-and-white saddle shoes, and a big flared skirt with a quilted pink poodle on it. Her hair was in a high ponytail. When the music started, she spun around and the skirt flew out in a wide circle. Astro was spinning, too.

The routine was amazing. They did some of the same moves they had done at Caring Paws, but Lizzie's jaw dropped when she saw some of the other things Astro could do, like walk backward on his hind legs and walk sideways.

"How can a dog even *do* that?" Mom gasped. "Dogs don't normally walk sideways. That is totally amazing."

"I bet Rusty could do it," said Lizzie, "if I just had enough time to train him." She snuck a look at her mom.

"Lizzie," Mom said. "Do I really have to remind you how fostering works?" She shook her head. "Our first priority has to be finding Rusty a good home, right?"

Lizzie's shoulders drooped. "Right," she said. She remembered about the family who was coming the next day to meet Rusty. Then she looked back at the computer screen. "But can we watch just a few more videos?" She pointed to one. "Laureen even has some training tips on this one. Maybe Rusty and I will have time to learn to do at least a few things together."

CHAPTER NINE

Lizzie set her alarm clock to wake her up extra early the next morning. When it went off, she groaned and rolled over. But Rusty jumped up and shook himself off, then licked her face as he stood over her on the bed.

Come on! We've got so much to do. Let's not waste any time.

"Okay, okay," said Lizzie. She lay there for a second, going over in her mind the things she'd learned from Laureen's training video the night before. It wasn't hard to teach a dog to back up, but it could take some time. You had to take it in small steps and keep the dog excited about what he was learning. There were lots of ways to do it—Lizzie had checked some other videos besides Laureen's—but she liked Laureen's technique best.

She pulled on her camp T-shirt and a pair of jeans, then headed downstairs with Rusty at her heels. She grabbed a stick of string cheese out of the fridge—Laureen had mentioned that extra-good treats were helpful—and they headed out into the backyard.

After she'd let him run for a while and do his business, Lizzie called Rusty over to stand in front of her. "Good boy," she said when she had his attention. Then she held a piece of the string cheese in her open palm and gently moved her palm under his chin. He took a step back so that he could take the cheese from her hand. "Good *boy*!" Lizzie said. It worked exactly as it had in Laureen's video. The dog had to back up to get the treat, and that way he could begin to learn what she wanted him to do.

She worked with Rusty for a few more minutes. Aunt Amanda always said that short training sessions were best, and that you should end on a good note. When Rusty took three steps back, Lizzie praised him and gave him another big piece of cheese. Then she got down on her knees and petted him until his wagging tail was a blur.

In the video, Laureen had shown how eventually Astro would back up as far as she wanted him to, with nothing but a tiny hand signal as a command. Lizzie still thought it was pretty amazing, but now she knew that almost any dog could learn how to do it. And a smart dog like Rusty would learn it very quickly; she was sure of that.

When she and Rusty arrived at Caring Paws that morning, Lizzie was bursting to tell Ms. Dobbins what Rusty had learned to do.

"That's wonderful," said Ms. Dobbins as she walked Lizzie and Rusty back to his kennel. "I can't wait to see you two demonstrate. But right now I have something else I want to talk to you about."

"Okay," said Lizzie, curious.

"This morning, the other campers will be sewing dog beds and spending some time reading stories to our new kittens—but I'm wondering if you'd like to do something different," Ms. Dobbins began. "You've been so helpful with Rusty that I thought you've earned the privilege of sitting in with me as I meet with the family I told you about, then introduce them to Rusty."

"Wow," said Lizzie. "I'd love to do that."

"There's only one thing," said Ms. Dobbins.

"You'll just be there as an observer, so you can see how I handle these interviews. We'll see how everyone gets along, and then we'll all make the decision together—but I want you to keep your thoughts to yourself during the meeting."

Lizzie nodded. "I will," she said, crossing her heart. "I promise."

The family arrived a few minutes later, and Ms. Dobbins brought them to her office for a quick interview before they met the adoptable dogs. Lizzie liked the Garcias right away. The dad was funny and kind, and the mom was sweet. The kids—three boys ages five to nine—were bursting with energy and noise, even though they were on their best behavior. The whole family seemed to be really excited about getting a dog. "We've had dogs before," the mom explained. "In fact, we just lost our old golden retriever a few

69

months ago. We've all been so sad about Rosie, but now we've decided we're ready for another pet."

Ms. Dobbins looked over their application and asked them a lot of questions, like whether they had a fenced yard (they did) and whether they were ready to take care of a dog's grooming and medical needs (they were, even when she pointed out that a dog with a long coat like Rusty's would require lots of grooming). "Well, then," she said when she had gone through all four pages of their application with them, "are you ready to meet some dogs?"

The boys jumped up and ran for the door. Lizzie smiled at the parents. "I can tell they love dogs," she said. That didn't count as sharing her thoughts, did it? She shot a quick look at Ms. Dobbins, who was also smiling.

The boys would have raced into the kennels, but their parents grabbed their hands and slowed them down. "Let's be very gentle and quiet with the dogs, all right?" the mom reminded them. "We don't want to scare them."

Lizzie helped take Rusty out of his kennel and into the yard, where there was more space for everyone to meet. "Wow," said the dad as he watched Rusty run. "He's quite an athlete, isn't he?"

"He definitely will need a lot of exercise," Ms. Dobbins agreed. "If you're looking for a couch potato, a dog like Rusty is not for you."

"We're both runners," said the mom. "And I love to run with a buddy."

Ms. Dobbins and Lizzie shared a look and a nod. Even though Lizzie couldn't stand the thought of giving him up so soon, she couldn't help admitting that the family seemed just right for Rusty. With three boys to give him attention, he would never be bored, and their energy level matched his perfectly.

Lizzie decided to show them how smart Rusty was. "Come, Rusty," she said, digging into her pocket for more string cheese. He heard the wrapper crinkle and galloped over, ears flapping.

I like that stuff! I'll do whatever you want as long as you keep it coming.

"Good boy," said Lizzie, praising him for coming when he was called. She gave him a hunk of cheese as he stood in front of her. Then she put another hunk in her palm and gently moved her hand under his chin. "Back up," she said. Rusty backed up—three whole steps!

"Whoa," said one of the boys.

Lizzie grinned. "Rusty loves to learn," she told him. "I bet you could teach him to back up across a whole football field." She hated to see Rusty go, but this family would give him a good home—and that was what fostering was all about.

CHAPTER TEN

The next morning, Lizzie got up early again to work with Rusty. It was so much fun to see his progress. He was definitely getting the idea. He began to back up as soon as Lizzie started to move her hand toward his chin. She got him up to four backward steps—then five!—before her mom called into the backyard that it was time to head to Caring Paws for her last day of camp.

"Coming," she called back. "One sec." She picked up the brush she'd left on the deck stairs and gave Rusty's coat a quick grooming. She wanted him to look his absolute best when the Garcias came to pick him up. They had left without making a final decision the day before but had promised Ms. Dobbins that they would be back in the morning. Lizzie was pretty sure they were going to take him.

It turned out that she was wrong.

When Lizzie arrived at camp, Ms. Dobbins was in the reception area to meet her. "Guess what," she said. "The Garcias have already been here to pick up the dog they decided on."

"But . . . Rusty's with me," said Lizzie, confused. She looked down at the happy dog by her side. He grinned up at her and wagged his tail.

Ms. Dobbins nodded. "They took Nora," she said. "They met her just before they left yesterday, and the whole family fell in love. I think she reminds them of their old dog who just died. Plus, they knew nobody else was likely to take her anytime soon." She sighed. "Such nice people. All I need is about a dozen more families like

Sammy shrugged. "Well, we're only in second grade," he said with a grin. "That girl was a senior in high school."

"Exactly," said Charles's dad, from the driver's seat. He met Charles's eyes in the mirror. "When you're a high school senior, you can invent some new way for people to communicate, or fly into space. But for now, I'm sure Mr. Mason will be happy with—I don't know—maybe a project on raising tadpoles."

Charles and Sammy cracked up. "No he won't!" said Sammy. "He made a rule this year: no tadpoles."

"He said he'll be happy if he never sees another tadpole again," Charles added. "He said he's had six years of tadpoles and that's enough." Mr. Mason was always saying funny things. He was the best teacher ever, and Charles really wanted to make him proud by doing a great project for the Littleton Elementary school science fair. That's why he and his best friend Sammy had convinced Charles's dad to take them to the high school science fair. They'd been hoping to find some inspiration there, but instead Charles just felt overwhelmed. All the projects were so impressive.

"Did you see that robot?" he asked Sammy. "The one that could shoot a basketball into a hoop?"

"Everybody's doing robots lately," Sammy said, shrugging. "I heard Jason is building a robot for our science fair."

"Yeah, from a kit his dad bought for him," said Charles. "All that shows is that he can follow directions. That guy tonight invented his whole robot from scratch! I think he's going to enter it in a national robotics competition."

that, and I'd have homes for all the animals at Caring Paws."

Lizzie looked at Ms. Dobbins. "It's great about Nora," she said. "But Rusty really needs a home, too." Once she had gotten used to the idea of giving Rusty up, Lizzie knew it was best if someone adopted him soon. Rusty was ready for a forever home.

Ms. Dobbins nodded. "I have an idea about that," she said, smiling. "But I'll need your help."

The last day of camp was a blast. Lizzie loved the craft project, which was making posters about being kind to animals. Lizzie had drawn a picture of a dog tied outside a house on a snowy day, with the caption *Don't leave your best friend out in the cold*. At lunchtime, they had a special treat of ice cream, donated by a local scoop shop. And they played some really fun games, like Who Am I?, where each camper had a sign taped to their back that told which animal they were. You had to ask other campers questions to figure out which animal you were. Lizzie was an otter, her favorite wild animal. She guessed it pretty quickly, since she knew so much about them.

After lunch, Ms. Dobbins let Lizzie have a little special time with Rusty, to brush him again and work some more on his training. It was all part of the plan. Rusty had to look his best and also be able to show off what a fast learner he was.

At the end of the day, it was time for the final event of camp. Instead of everyone going home, the campers' families came to Caring Paws to join them for a big pizza party. All the special guests from the last three days were invited, too: Aunt Amanda, the vet and the vet techs, and Laureen.

According to the plan she and Ms. Dobbins had made, Lizzie sat next to Laureen after she'd gotten herself a soda and a slice of pizza. "I love the videos you posted online," Lizzie said. "You and Astro have such an amazing partnership."

Laureen smiled. "There's nothing like it," she said. "I love training dogs, and Astro loves learning. We have so much fun together."

"I've been working with one of the dogs here," said Lizzie. "He's an Irish setter."

"Ooh," said Laureen. "I love setters. Those beautiful coats!"

"His name is Rusty," Lizzie went on. "He is beautiful—and really smart, too. You'll see when I do my demo."

After pizza, the families roamed around looking at the campers' artwork and crafts. Then each camper gave a short presentation about something they'd learned during the week. One girl talked about cat care, and another camper showed the poster he'd made about animal adoption.

Nicole's presentation was about dog grooming, and she brought one of the shelter pups, a pretty cocker spaniel named Fifi, into the meeting room to show off her work. Nicole had been sad to see her Pet Pal Nora go, but she was thrilled that Nora had found such a loving home.

"For our next presentation, by Lizzie Peterson, we'll go out to the dog yard," said Ms. Dobbins.

Lizzie raced ahead of the crowd to get Rusty. "Ready, pal?" she asked. Rusty wagged his tail and gave his floppy ears a shake.

You know it! I love to show off.

Lizzie gave Rusty a few extra swipes with the brush until his coat was gleaming, then snapped on his leash and led him outside. In a few moments, the crowd of campers, their families, and friends had gathered. Lizzie looked at Laureen, standing next to Ms. Dobbins. When Laureen saw Rusty, she mouthed a big "Wow!" and gave Lizzie a thumbs-up.

Lizzie felt butterflies in her stomach. She knew that Rusty had learned a lot, but he could still be a little wild and distracted—especially when he hadn't had a chance to run around the yard. She looked down at him, and he gazed back at her. The trusting look in his big brown eyes melted away all her fears.

Let's show them what we can do!

Lizzie patted her left thigh, and Rusty fell into place next to her. They walked around in a big circle and then did some figure eights. Rusty stuck to Lizzie like glue, watching her closely for clues about which direction to go. "Good boy," she kept saying as she slipped him bits of the special freeze-dried liver treats she had brought. Then it was time to show off his best trick. She wheeled around so that he was standing in front of her. "Back up, Rusty," she said.

Rusty backed up—six whole steps!

The crowd went wild, hooting and applauding as Lizzie took a bow. She grinned down at Rusty. "What a good boy," she said. When she looked up, Laureen was standing next to her.

"This dog is a natural," she said, bending over to give Rusty a pat. "I'd give anything to work with him. Astro and I would love for Rusty to join our family."

Lizzie's grin grew wider. "That's exactly what we were hoping for," she said as Ms. Dobbins joined them.

"You're a natural, too," Laureen told Lizzie. "I can see that you really love working with dogs.

Would you like to help me train Rusty in freestyle?"

Lizzie stared at her. "Really?" she asked. "I can't think of anything I'd like better." She reached down to stroke Rusty's silky ears. The beautiful red pup had found the perfect home.

THE PUPPY PLACE

DON'T MISS THE NEXT PUPPY PLACE ADVENTURE!

Here's a peek at ROXY

"Did you see the girl who was explaining her experiment on how mushrooms can save the planet?" Sammy asked. "That was so cool."

Charles nodded. "She made a whole movie about it and everything." He sighed. "I don't think our science fair projects are going to come anywhere close to that," he said.

ABOUT THE AUTHOR

Ellen Miles loves dogs, which is why she has a great time writing the Puppy Place books. And guess what? She loves cats, too! (In fact, her very first pet was a beautiful tortoiseshell cat named Jenny.) That's why she came up with the Kitty Corner series. Ellen lives in Vermont and loves to be outdoors with her dog, Zipper, every day, walking, biking, skiing, or swimming, depending on the season. She also loves to read, cook, explore her beautiful state, play with dogs, and hang out with friends and family.

Visit Ellen at ellenmiles.net.

Dear Reader,

I can't believe I have written so many Puppy Place books (over 50!) and I haven't written about freestyle/dancing with dogs before. I learned about this sport long ago when my friend Jody and her dog Scout began working on a routine. Scout was a Gordon setter who looked very much like Rusty, with a flowing red coat. I've never forgotten how beautiful Scout looked as she and Jody danced together and how cool it was to see the bond that they shared.

Yours from the Puppy Place,

Ellen Miles

P.S. For another book about a talented and high-spirited dog, check out *Sweetie*.

PUPPY TIPS

There are so many activities to do with your dog, from doggy dancing to agility to dock diving. Some dogs love to catch Frisbees, and others love to use their noses, practicing their tracking skills. Every dog has different talents, and some of these activities can be wonderful bonding opportunities for you and your pet. But what your dog wants most of all is to spend time with you, whether you're playing, taking a walk, or just snuggling on the couch. Be sure to make time for your dog every day!

"Robot, bobot, dobot," sang the Bean from his car seat. "Beep, beep, beep!"

"That's right!" said Charles, holding up a hand to give his little brother a high five. "Robots say beep-beep."

"Boop-boop," said the Bean, laughing his gurgly laugh. "Goop-goop. Zeep-zeep."

Charles and Sammy cracked up again. Charles was glad Dad had decided to bring the Bean along, even if it meant that they'd had to walk very slowly through the science fair. It was always fun to go places with the Bean, because everyone loved him. He got a lot of attention. It was sort of like having a cute puppy along.

"Lizzie would have liked that exhibit on how to measure dog intelligence," said Charles. His older sister was totally dog-crazy. "She would have been impressed by that border collie who knew over two hundred words."

"I think I'm glad that Buddy isn't quite that smart," said Dad. "Your Aunt Amanda always says that dogs who are too smart can be trouble."

Charles laughed. He was thankful that Buddy had been smart enough, and cute enough, and charming enough, to make the whole Peterson family fall in love with him when he first came to them as a foster puppy. Unlike all the other puppies they had fostered, who had only stayed a short time, Buddy had stayed forever, becoming part of the family.